donated to

North Beverly School

Beverly, Massachusetts

by Brianna Nestor

in honor of

Mrs. Sherriff

8560

Cousin Ruth's Tooth

by AMY MacDONALD

Illustrations by MARJORIE PRICEMAN

Houghton Mifflin Company
Boston 1996

For Thomas
—A. M.

For Tracey, Annie, and Trudy
—M. P.

For information about this and other Houghton Mifflin
trade and reference books and multimedia products,
visit The Bookstore at Houghton Mifflin on the World
Wide Web at http://www.hmco.com/trade/.

Manufactured in the United States of America

The text of this book is set in Century Schoolbook.
The illustrations are watercolor, reproduced in full color.

WOZ   10   9   8   7   6   5   4   3   2   1

Library of Congress Cataloging-in-Publication Data
MacDonald, Amy.
Cousin Ruth's tooth / by Amy MacDonald ; illustrated by
Marjorie Priceman.
      p.   cm.
Summary: When little Cousin Ruth loses a tooth, the whole
Fister family is in a dither.
ISBN 0-395-71253-X
[1. Teeth—Fiction.   2. Stories in rhyme.]
I. Priceman, Marjorie, ill.   II. Title.
PZ8.3.M1315Co   1996   94-26426
[E]—dc20   CIP AC

"Rachel Fister,
get your sister!"
Mrs. Fister spread the word.

"Cousin Ruth has
lost a tooth! O,
careless youth! It's too absurd.

"Never mind it!
We shall find it!
We will search both low and high."

4

"Well," said Ruth, "to
  tell the truth, I—"
"Hush now, darling, don't you cry.

"Find your cousins
—several dozens—
Get your uncles and your aunts:

"Bess! Matilda!
Olga! Zelda!
Mary Lee and Uncle Lance!

"Uncle Walter!
  Never falter.
  Search the cellar, check the roof.

"Norma Jean and
Aunt Bodine,
go check the attic for the tooth.

9

"Search the yard and
search the garden.
Check the engine of the car.

"Check the hatbox.
Check the cat box.
Look inside the VCR.

"Faster! Harder!
Search the larder.
Check the pockets of your pants.

"Harder! Faster!"
"Quelle disaster!"
(said Aunt Bea, who'd been to France).

Though they searched in ways most ruthless,
after days they still were...toothless.

"This adventure
of the denture's
quickly fixed," said Uncle Drew.

"Yes, forsooth! I'll
buy a tooth! I'll
stick it on with Super Glue!"

"Go to Wal-Mart,
Sears, and All-Mart,"
cried the youngest cousin, Keith.

"L. L. Bean!"
cried Norma Jean.
"Oh, someone's *bound* to have some teeth!"

17

Uncle Rickie
grabbed a stick; he
said, "I'll whittle one real quick!"

Auntie May said,
"One from clay! I'll
make it now—this very day!"

19

"We've been burgled!"
Aunt Bea gurgled.
"Call the army, call the p'lice!

"Someone stole her
little molar!
Someone's robbed my little niece!"

21

Mrs. Fister
hushed her sister,
said to Ruthie, "In this clan,

"we're the Fisters
—misses, misters—
and we *always* have a plan!

"For this dental
matter, mental
fortitude is what we need.

"Ask the wisest
to advise us."
Ask the Queen, they all agreed.

So they faxed her
and they asked her.
Her reply was brief: "You goons!

"Of this dental
incident, I'll
say just this: TIME HEALS ALL WOUNDS!"

27

"What does it mean?"
mused Aunt Bodine,
and Cousin Bess, and Uncle Max.

Said Ruth, "Look here—"
"Not now, my dear.
We're trying to figure out this fax."

"*Ahem*," said Ruth.

"I FOUND MY TOOTH!"

and opened up for all to see.

"There's another,"
  gasped her brother,
"where the other used to be!"

"Did you ever!
  Aren't you clever!"
  cried the Fisters. "Silly child!

"Such a fuss you
caused for us!"
But little Ruthie simply...smiled.